I0534433

Treasure at Shepherds Pass

Alex Mitchell

Published by Alex Mitchell, 2023.

This is a work of fiction. Similarities to real people, places, or events are entirely coincidental.

TREASURE AT SHEPHERDS PASS

First edition. October 9, 2023.

ISBN: 979-8891980020

Written by Alex Mitchell.

Also by Alex Mitchell

Revenge at Shepherds Pass
Treasure at Shepherds Pass
Welcome to Shepherds Pass

Chapter 1

On a warm August day in 1953, four men entered the Roosevelt Federal Bank in St. Louis with the intent of robbing the bank. They made a series of miscalculations that would lead to a trail of dead bodies and set off treasure hunts that would end only generations later. The four men were Erwin Appleton, George Toole, Bolden Tucker, and Melvin Price. Their leader was Erwin Appleton. They had met in the army and had decided to apply their crafts they had learned to one bank job, separate then meet a year later and split the proceeds.

According to the FBI Unified Crime Report, a collection of facts and figures documented by the FBI utilizing a collection of information from all the charted police forces in the United States, the more bank robbers successfully commit a robbery the higher the chances they will be caught. The FBI uses patterns and methods to track bank robbers. One robbery leaves little pattern. Also, according to FBI data if the bank robbers leave with the proceeds from the bank between 22% and 25% is never returned. Elroy Price, Melvin Price's younger brother had been recruited to drive the getaway van. The first item of major consequence of miscalculation was not completely foreseeable. Banks hold a set number of receipts at the bank and send excess amounts of receipts to the Federal Reserve.

Due to a merger, there were excessive amounts held at the bank they entered being prepared to be sent out to the Federal Reserve. This meant that instead of the 200,000 they had estimated they would steal they found themselves standing in front of over 281,000,000.00. Many of the banks involved in the merger had gold double eagle coins and 1000.00 bills that were being taken out of circulation.

The second miscalculation of significant consequence was the large number of guards. These men had never worked together which gave the small team of four trained soldiers who had recently returned from the battlefield a huge advantage leading to the blood bath as guards, of whom had never fired their weapons in close combat lost their lives.

The next consequence involved Erwin Appleton who after hiding the money where only he would know where it was returned home and found his next-door neighbor in his bed having sex with his wife. Appleton took the gun he had just used in multiple homicidal bank robberies and shot his wife and neighbor to death. Appleton was convicted of two counts of murder and put in the penitentiary. Several years into Appleton's stay in the pen the FBI decided to update its database of ballistics and in doing so matched the weapon used in the Roosevelt Federal job to Appleton.

The funds from the Roosevelt job were not recovered when Appleton was charged, and a host of deal-making began.

APPLETON CONVICTED had been for the robbery and the murders and given life in prison. Yet still another unfortunate event shaped the future treasure hunt. In a prison gang rumble, in which Appleton was not involved directly involved; was caught in the middle and sustained severe brain damage. His ability to remember was destroyed.

"Gee, this Crap is nasty." Doris Fleischman commented making a face the reveal how vile she thought the green energy drink was.

"Mine tastes like toxic waste; it's got to be good for you," Abby responded. The two women had just left a workout session at Galaxy Plus Gym in Shepherds Pass. Doris and Abby had been working out together since they met at the tables of Alcoholics Anonymous.

"Walk with me to my car, Sister." Doris requested.

The parking lot had several cars parked but there were no people present. Doris opened the door of her rusted Nissan and reached for the back seat. She retrieved a small English Bulldog puppy that looked too young to be away from his mother. Doris handed it to Abby who looked shocked.

"What is this?"

"It's a dog."

"Why are you giving me a dog? I don't even know if I like dogs."

"He is a puppy, so I guess the two of you have time to work it out."

"What?"

The puppy opened his eyes and gave Abby a sad stare. He blinked as if having trouble focusing then pushed with his head to nuzzle against Abby.

"Looks like love at first sight to me. Look girl, I owe you money. The chessedick that breeds these puppies owed me money, so he gave me the puppy."

"So, you keep him."

"Can't, they won't allow it in my apartment. You can sell him and make a profit."

Both women rested against the car for the moment enjoying the August breeze. "Does he have a name?"

"Tell me again about the dream you keep having that makes you nervous." Doris seemed to be ignoring Abby's question.

"THERE I WAS IN MY APARTMENT and the country guy I work with walked into the room. He slings me on the bed and rips my clothes off. He screws me every which way possible. No words, nothing. Then he walks out."

"I thought you like men that are basic."

"I don't even know if I like this guy. And I don't think he likes me. But wow it's so real."

While the girls are talking a red Challenger hellcat drives up and two guys are staring at Doris. She knew them.

"How's that ass, Dottie?" A stingy-haired guy with a narrow face and five o'clock shadows asked, eyeing Doris.

"I'm good. Scott." Scott surveyed the area as if trying to see who might be watching.

"Hand me my purse?" Abby requested Doris. Doris reached into the car and reappeared with the purse and handed it to Abby who was under inspection by the two men in the challenger. Abby noticed the strong smell of marijuana at about the same time she noticed the blue van approaching. Abby, being a police detective, did not like the way the van stopped and blocked the Nissan. It was not by accident that the two groups of guys had blocked their departure.

"Is your friend up for the game?" Scott asked Doris.

"No way she's a straight girl and so am I now."

"Fuck that get in the van."

The door to the van slid open and four guys stepped out. They all had handguns in their waistbands. Abby adjusted her position to get a clear field of vision between herself and the group developing. Abby's training as a cop was moving her around as if on autopilot. Something bad was unfolding. No stopping it now. Only minimize the damage. Abby looked back over her shoulder hoping someone was watching.

"Look she doesn't want to go," Abby stated.

"What's the puppy's name?" The oldest man from the van addressed Abby.

"Cletus."

They all laughed.

"Don't laugh at his name you might hurt his feelings."

"Shouldn't he be wearing suspenders or something?"

Eric, the older of the team asked.

"Dottie this bitch is crazier than you are." Scott assessed.

Scott reached into the challenger and pulled out a .357 and pointed it at Dottie. "You know there is only one way for this to end."

At the click of Scott cocking the hammer of the colt python Abby fired and shot Scott in the center of his forehead. This did not however stop Scott's gun from firing and shooting Doris in the head and spaying Abby and Cletus with blood, scull fragments, and what appeared to be brain matter.

"Police," Abby screamed flipping the puppy into the back of the Nissan. One of the crew from the van drew his gun and Abby shot him center mass and he fell backward into the oldest man. Abby looked out of the corner of her eye and found herself staring down the shaky barrel of a gun she spun as her training took over again and she fired. The gun facing her fired the bullet shot slightly past her head as her shot went into the chest of the shooter. She ducked behind a parked car as the driver of the hellcat revved the engine with the demonic howl it manufactures. The other men were piling into the van. Abby jumped up and shot through the out-the-back window of the escaping hellcat as the van took off as well. Abby heard the mournful cry of Doris lying in a pool of her blood. Abby put her finger in Doris's blood and wrote down the last three numbers from the escaping hell cat and the last three from the van.

"Don't cry, Sister. All I want is to die sober. I might get my wish." Doris coughed and expelled blood. A crowd had appeared out of nowhere watching the mayhem.

"One of you motherfuckers dial 911," Abby yelled at the top of her lungs. Abby retrieved Cletus from the car, and he seemed to take it as his job to cheer her up, but this was not completely possible.

Chapter 3

"Shootouts and dead bodies getting to be a thing with you isn't it, Detective Blackwell?" Detron Clark, the paramedic, stated as he was attempting to stabilize Doris. The Emergency Medical Unit arrived at the same time as the uniformed police. Wendell Bishop a uniformed officer who has recently passed the sergeant's examinations and was in the process of being assigned as a sergeant answered the call with his partner Office Webber. Webber was a strong athletic woman who wore her uniform Proudly.

"Fuck you Detron."

"We did that dance as I recall it was right nice." Detron chuckled. Detron was a tall slender black man in a paramedic uniform and dreadlocks. He looked like he could run out onto any football field or baseball field and outperform any star that had been playing that day.

"I got to go with her," Abby announced.

"Procedure states you stay here," Wendell informed Abby.

"Kiss my ass. Don't tell me the policy."

"Abby, Nash, and Lopez are in route it's their seen. I am a temporary sergeant even though the paperwork has not yet been cleared."

Abby walked up to Wendell and stood directly in front of him. She still held the shaking puppy covered in blood.

"I outrank you."

"You are part of a crime scene. You are a victim."

"You want to see who a victim is?"

"Abby get out of his face or I will bag your ass myself," Webber commanded. Webber was a uniformed female cop that usually assisted Wendell, they were close friends off work as well.

Wendell looked around like he knew it was up to him to compromise or everything would get out of hand. "Okay here's the play. You voluntarily hand over your weapon to me right here and now. And you ride to the hospital with the girl that was shot. Webber is with you at all times until Lopez and Nash say otherwise." Wendell looked over at Webber. "Officer you are with her at all times. That means that if he has to go take a piss, I want you to be able to tell me if Fuzzy wuzzy was a bear or if fuzzy wuzzy had no hair."

"This aint over Bishop." Abby protested and unloaded her gun and handed it to Wendell.

In minutes the ambulance was underway. Webber looked at Abby. "Just for the record if you ever disrespect that man in the field again, I am going to put my foot so far up your as you will smell polish every time you take a breath for the rest of your nasty ass life."

"Anytime you feel froggish, Butch. Feel free to hop right over."

Detron beat on the divider glass to get the driver's attention. "Hey, speed it up give me lights and sirens all the way. I think a war is about to break out back here."

Chapter 4

"Doctor, I think you are right. Nya commented to Doctor Floyd as they walked toward their cars.

"Thank you for helping in the children's ward. They love you so much you make being there fun for them."

Nya froze for a second as a shiver ran down her back. What is it? Something is about to unfold. Within seconds a blue van pulled up and a young man barely out of his teens stepped out carrying a gun and pointed it at Dr. Floyd. "Are you a doctor?"

"Yes."

"Good, get in the van."

"I'm not going anywhere with you." The words were barely out of the doctor's mouth before he was struck twice in the head by the gun. The doctor dropped to his knees and the young man put the gun to his temple.

"Then you aint no good to me."

An older rougher looking man stepped out of the van and walked over to Nya. "My name is Eric and a couple of my people need help. Will you help us?"

"Will you tell him not to pull the trigger?" Nya asked.

"Deal." Eric nodded and the kid lowered the gun and kicked Doctor Floyd.

Eric rolled back the door of the van. Inside you could see that at least two of the men were bleeding. One was unconscious and one held his chest and blood oozed through his finger.

"Take the doctor's backpack he has things we will need." Indicating the backpack, the fallen doctor was carrying. Nya rushed into the van, and it was off before the door had fully closed.

"I and never fucked a Nigger Bitch before." Came from one of the guys in the van.

"Now here this. No one uses that word again or I will cut off your nuts. No one touches her or stares at her too long or I will cut off your nuts. If any of you show disrespect to her and I cut off your nuts." Eric announced.

"Why so rough boss." The kid asked.

"Because you have never been in prison, and I have. She sacrificed herself to save her friend. People with honor respect people with honor. In the joint or outside it's how shit is supposed to work. Or you set bad shit in motion." Eric answered without looking at Nya or Brendan the young thug.

"There is a pen and paper in the backpack hand it to me," Nya yelled at the kid holding the backpack as she examined the guy with the chest wound. "What is your name?" Nya asked. Examining the guy Abby had shot, who would otherwise have shot Abby in the head.

"Joey."

"Well Joey, I think you have good capillary blanching which means you most likely will not lose this arm if you do what I tell you. Are you on board with that?" Fearlessly Nya stared into the face of the thug.

"You call the tune. I dance. Got it."

"Is this the hand you use with you fire a gun?"

"Yes."

"Then you may have to learn to shoot with the other hand. You may suffer some motor loss without surgery. Reaction time in this arm could be slower than you are used to."

"How would I get surgery?"

"The surgeon was the guy your friend was about to shoot in the head."

"If that is your way of telling me to help keep him on a chain? Point taken." Joey smiled.

"How long before we get where we are going? We are bouncing this poor guy to death." Nya asked examining the guy that lye unconscious.

"We are almost there," Eric answered.

The van pulled into an abandoned yard where a trucking transport company was once housed. Nya continued examining the guy on the floor of the van after the men were exiting. She began scribbling on the pad and handed it to Brendan.

"I want you to bring these things back to me. Do not get them all in the same place. I need you back here in ten minutes. If you don't have everything, then come back and give me what you have, and go again. Do you understand?" Brendan stared at her not accustomed to taking orders from a woman.

"Why can't I get it all in the same place?"

"Because you idiot it would be easy for the police to track what you bought and pick your young ass up. Which means Jay will die from your stupidity. She is trying to help you not get caught. Brendan nodded as if now became able to follow Eric's instructions. This left his communication skills crippled.

"Do you hear me," Nya yelled in Brendan's face.

"Yeah, lady." Brendan looked around possibly for support from Calvin, but it was clear by the way Calvin was looking at Nya his mind had drifted someplace else.

"Good because this guy's life is in my hands and you are not going to fuck that up, are you?"

"No, lady."

Eric smiled, not sure where the source of Nya's courage came from but happy, she was holding it together.

After Brendan had scampered off Eric leaned close to Nya to help move the wounded man to the building. "Is he going to make it?"

Nya looked at Eric in such a way that let him know he wanted him to be clear on her next statement.

"Unconscious People can sometimes not be able to communicate but can hear everything you say. So, we are going to give him all the encouragement that we can muster." Nya's arm touched Eric and she shuddered again then she took his palm and looked at his hand. "That's why you aren't scared you are some kind of witch or something."

Nya looked at her patient ignoring Eric's statement.

"What is his name?"

"Jay Bone, he's, my brother." Eric's answer was short but filled with emotional trigger points.

"So, from now on we call him by name and include him in any major conversation, deal."

"Deal."

Chapter 5

"We need to talk. Noreen announced to Lavon as they sat at the dining table. Lavon Tyler had been staying with his girlfriend Judge Lynn Dodd Masterson after being injured on the job as a police detective. Lavon and Noreen had a kitchen table full of brochures with home listings in the area. Lavon was diligently examining the selection and failed to notice that Noreen had stopped looking at flyers and was watching him.

"Anything little bit."

"See that's the first problem." A quizzical look overtook Lavon's face.

"You see me as a little girl and that's fine most of the time. Brothers always see little sisters as children. But I am a woman."

"You aren't going to talk dirty, are we? You know how it makes my stomach hurt when you girls walk nasty in front of me." The Tyler's had lived in Lamont Mississippi and spoke with a discernible accent.

They sat in the dining room of Lynn's semi mansion unclear on how to address the adult issue she wanted to discuss.

"Okay here goes. Since you can here to live how many nights have you woke up and Lynn was here in the house, and she was sleeping in a different bed than you." It was clear that Lavon knew the answer, but he was not sure if he wanted to answer, not knowing what her next question would be. Noreen was in school to become a Lawyer and was smart.

"None."

"But you told me she gave you your room."

13

"Yes, she did."

"Then she is sleeping with you out of need and desire, not utility. Don't treat her like a utility or she will shit on you one day. She wakes up wrapped in your love every morning. She came to you when you needed her most and now you seem in a rush to push that aside as if it won't change anything."

"Are you saying I shouldn't move out?"

"I am saying whatever you do make it a decision the two of you agree to, for some reason she loves you. You, blockhead, accept that and work from there."

Lavon found himself hugging his sister when his cell phone rang.

"TYLER, YOUR PARTNER is becoming our designated gunslinger." Lieutenant Crawford informed him as Lavon answered Designated Gunslinger is a mythical term used for a cop who is often put in a situation where a shootout is inevitable. The gunslinger gets to kill the bad guy often because the cops know the evidence, they have on the perpetrator won't hold up in court.

"How many?"

"At least two but the count could go up."

"Where is she?"

"Not why I called. We have a person snatched from the parking lot of Shepard General Hospital."

"Wow, boss you are full of good news."

"It gets better. The girl grabbed is Nya Dubois."

"Does Wendell know?"

"Not yet I have been using him to fill in as a sergeant. I am going to pull him in-house on a blind call and hope no one lets the cat out of the bag before I get a chance to talk to him. Be ready to catch him if need be."

"Remember to show her the dignity of letting her be part of the choice when or if you move out," Noreen yelled to her brother as he left.

Chapter 6

"I feel like such a coward." Dr. Floyd stated from his hospital bed. Lavon had arrived at the hospital and viewed the tape of the parking lot confrontation. Lavon had set the sketch artist to get a picture of the perpetrators. He radioed the description of the van to local street patrols.

"Don't. It is proven that young people often don't have a clear view of life and death. To them, it's a game."

"You sound like you have been involved in this type of thing before." Dr. Floyd looked frail and tired beyond his years. "Will you find her?"

"Count on it."

Walking down the hallway of the hospital Lavon spotted Rena Lopez and Don Nash the Detectives that had caught the shooting in front of the Galaxy Plus Gym.

"How is my partner?" Lavon asked.

"Stupid. Loud. Hard to get along with. Other than that, fine." Lopez answered.

"She doesn't care if she works with us or not. That is going to create a problem. The shooting review is not going to hang her, but they won't be happy she killed more people." Nash added. Nash was the calm slow talking type of Detective that did not mind that you knew he was always assessing you.

"You think she is keeping secrets?"

"Most likely. I just hope it doesn't come back to bite us all." Lopez expressed.

"I got an abduction from the hospital parking lot. Blue van. That mean anything to you two?"

"Bingo. Blue van in the shootout also a red challenger hellcat." Lopez answered.

"Hospitals got tapes from the cameras on the lots. You two might what to take a look." Lavon suggested.

"So why is it you know how to play with others in the sandbox and your partner does not?" Lopez was shorter than her partner with dark hair that hinted of Hispanic descent. She spoke clear English and kept her hair in the bun that female uniform cops usually wear.

"Where is she?" Lavon knew he finally had to ask.

"Break room down there. The girl. Doris Dottie Fleischman came through for a few moments and ask for the priest. So, your partner had to leave the room." Nash explained.

Lavon found Abby sitting on a sofa in the break room. Someone had given her a baby bottle of milk and she had Cletus wrapped in a baby blanket holding him like a newborn feeding him from the bottle. Lavon sat down without speaking and watched her for a moment waiting for her to start the conversation.

"Cletus this is your father." She finally said to the puppy.

"This Shepherds Pass is an amazing place. Why the Sam Hill would you name a dog Cletus?"

"Well, he reminds me of you."

An elderly lady wandered into the breakroom depending heavily on an aluminum cane. The woman walked close to where Lavon and Abby were sitting. Abby pulled back the blanket to let the lady get a good look. The old woman was expecting to see an infant.

"He's our first. I think he takes after his father's side of the family."

The lady looked shocked. "The big guy likes it doggy style so much this is what you get," Abby added. The woman propelled herself out of the room as fast as she could.

"Have you known Doris long?" Lavon asked.

"Are you working the case?"

"No, they don't want me to."

"She didn't deserve to die like that."

"You are giving up on her."

"Just accepting what's real. Remember I was there."

"I think your bad guys snatched Nya."

"Shit. Well, I guess I should tell you. I had a screaming match with Wendell and if he didn't hate my guts before he sure as hell does now."

"Well sounds like there is plenty of pity to go around but I am saving mine for Nya. I know what her chances are and what they can do to her. Things are even if we get her body back, we might not get her mind back."

After a moment of silence, the priest that worked in the hospital came into the breakroom. He handed a piece of paper to Abby.

"What this?"

"She has left this world to rest in a better place. She made her will out to you."

"That jerk she only owed me a few hundred dollars. No big deal."

"Then keep it for the memory. Did you have the same mother and father?" The priest asked.

"None of your business." Abby snapped. She stood and looked at Lavon. "Give me and the baby a ride home and we can practice not talking."

Lavon, Cletus, and Abby walked toward the exit to the hospital and Detective Lopez was waiting. "Detective Blackwell, do you mind if I speak privately with your partner for a moment?" The women exchanged evil glances for a moment before Abby spoke. "Come on baby we know when we are not wanted. We will wait outside."

"Abby if you keep talking to that dog like that, they are going to put you in a straitjacket and there aint a thing I can do about that," Lavon called as the pair left.

"I wanted to tell you a couple of things firsthand. You know how the rumor mill usually gets things half right." Lopez sounded different than their first encounter. She was now uncomfortable or even vulnerable. "I want to thank you for all the women of the squad for what you did to Lucas. Word is he may never be able to return to active duty."

Lavon chose the slight gap in her speaking to examine her face. She had more to say but it was coming uneasily. "I slept with him for a while. He had a thing where after the relationship, if you could call it that, broke up he humiliated you. You lost all self-respect. People you thought where your friend didn't want to see you coming." She stopped and swallowed.

"Lopez, you don't owe me an explanation. I did what I did because of what I am and what he is."

"I'M NOT THROUGH. ABBY was the worst of his toys." Lopez stopped and walked closer to Lavon as though proximity could convey the extreme nature of her next comment. "You are a soldier. You were in the military, and you have that no man left behind state of mind. There is another frame of mind you may need to adapt as a cop."

"What's that?"

"Never let a partner drag you under."

Lavon led Abby and Cletus across the hospital parking lot to his truck. Lavon could almost feel the heat from the confrontation earlier that day where the Doctor was beaten, and Nya was taken.

"Well, this is much better. Cowboy." Abby was surprised at the shiny new truck.

"Noreen came up to help me house hunt and dropped off my truck. She finally got her new car."

"So, you are moving out from the Judge."

"Don't quite know yet."

Cletus seemed to get jealous of Abby's purse sitting on her lap and grabbed it with his teeth and shook the purse causing the contents to fly out onto the floor of the truck. Abby leaned forward and began collecting the contents. "Here this is yours." She handed him a key.

"It's not mine."

"It was on the floor of your truck, and I don't recognize it, so it did not come out of my purse."

Lavon took the key and stuck it in his pocket. "Maybe my sister lost it, thank you."

The remainder of the ride home was quiet with Abby and Cletus sleeping until they were dropped off.

As Lavon headed back home, he kept thinking about how to best speak to Lynn about their living arrangements. He loved being there in her semi-mansion with her and Rosa her maid. But he was not sure it was the proper thing for him to do. Before he could resolve this issue, he was contacted by dispatch for the police station with an address telling him to meet the fire department there for a Viking Funeral. A term he had no clue as to what it meant.

Chapter 7

"This is Vinita Gonzalez for Chanel 2 new reporting from the scene of the car fire in a field just outside Shepherds Pass. The fire department has stopped the blaze but there appears to be a body inside the car. It is unclear if the person was killed before the fire or died as the result." Lavon saw the lights and the News truck. It had helped him find the area, but he was still unclear why he was there.

"Approaching us is Detective Lavon Tyler. Detective Tyler is the departmental sharpshooter who solved over seven murders and cracked a multi-million-dollar scam that threatened to cripple the economy of all Shepherd's Pass. He did this in less than a week."

Lavon wondered how the cute little Hispanic woman in heels could manage to move so fast as she raced to catch him before he was allowed behind the police line where she would not be allowed. She shoved a microphone in front of him and a cameraman directed the camera toward him.

"Detective, are you here to resolve the shooting that took place at Galaxy Plus Gym earlier today?" Gonzalez asked.

Lavon did not want any part of the sideshow that was in process, but he was desperate to help Nya. For her safety, he would play ball.

"No, ma'am not directly. Detectives Lopez and Nash are spearheading that investigation."

"They why are you here?"

"We had an assault followed by an abduction in front of Shepard General Hospital. A young lady was taken by force. She is in danger, and I am sure you and anyone else that encounters her abductor will help. Decent folks must rally together to come to the aid of their neighbors despite any small difference."

Gonzalez looked shocked; this was more conversation than she had ever gotten from a police officer in quite some time. "What can we do?"

"WELL, YOU CAN HELP by staying out of the way when possible. You can assist by answering questions when asked. And you can help by keeping this girl in your prayers, we want to get her home to her loved ones as soon as possible."

"What is her name?"

"Unfortunately, due to regulations it is not clear if her parents have been notified so we will release that part of the information as soon as possible but at this time we simply are not allowed to. Please excuse me." Lavon stepped beyond the yellow tape and walked over to a large heavyset man in a black fireman's jacket.

"Paul Simms, arson investigator, among other things." Paul offered his hand it was the size of a catcher's mitt.

"Why is it called a Viking funeral."

"The dead body is put in the vehicle; it is set on fire then rolled off a cliff or into a ditch and the guy lands in Valhalla."

"Poetic."

"We do our best. By the way, beware of that little hot tamale there. They are mad at you guys."

"Cops? What did we do?"

"You have been working cases and solving crime. With no leaks, or insider information and no juicy tidbits."

Lavon laughed as walked closer to the burned-out vehicle. It was what was left of the burned-out challenger hellcat. There were still the burned remains of a body inside and the coroner looked confused as to how to get it out of the car without causing further damage.

"Rear window was missing when the fire took place," Simms informed him he had walked up while Lavon was looking at the remains of the license plates. "Any insights."

"Yeah, one. This is the same group from the gunfight at the Gym. Somebody needed a doctor and had to settle for a nurse." Lavon informed.

"Hey, Tyler," Simms called to Lavon as he was leaving.

"Yeah."

"This year's charity boxing match. You guys lost your heavy weight, any chance you find someone to replace him in time?"

"Working on it."

Lavon had slept restlessly. When he woke up Lynn had left for work and he now lye there alone for a moment thinking how different his life was with Lynn near him. He thought about what Noreen had told him about waking up surrounded by the love of another. Lavon had suffered the recent breakup of an unfaithful girlfriend and now wondered if his plan to distance himself was an overreaction to hurt. He felt shame and embarrassment.

Lavon knew his family was always behind his decisions, but he needed distance from everything and everyone he knew.

In many respects, Shepherds Pass provided plenty of that.

Chapter 8

As he walked across the lot to the new police station, he noticed the
was a stocky girl in a leather jacket walking behind him. She was
following him but did not seem to care if he knew it.

"You aren't good at following people." Lavon finally turned around
and confronted her. The Woman had a pock-marked face with heavy eye
makeup and long stringy hair and was in the process of transitioning
from black to grey. Her breast was in a major cascade and drooping.

"I wanted you to know I was following you, Detective Tyler."

She sat on the steps and Lavon sat down beside her. "Do you mind if
I smoke?"

"If you have to."

"Asking was a formality dude." She reached into her jacket's inner
pocket and removed a pack of cigarettes and a lighter. She lit the cigarette
and took a long draw; she held the smoke. She seemed to look up as
though the smoke had a healing power then finally released the smoke.
She repeated the process, and half the cigarette was gone before she
seemed able to rejoin Lavon in conversation.

"My name is Roberta." She smiled and the yellow staining of her
teeth was no surprise to Lavon. Roberta's voice had a raspy gravely
quality like an aged rock singer.

"Do we know each other?"

"I am Abby's sponsor."

Now the conversation was starting to take shape. "I am concerned about Abby," Lavon confessed.

"Then we have something in common."

"She needs to stay sober for herself. Not for you or her job or the king."

"Am I interfering?"

"I don't think so, but I think you should get some help. Al-anon. A support group for family and loved ones of alcoholics. Learn not to be an enabler and how to accept disappointment."

Roberta's face had not changed, and she fired her second cigarette and smoked it with the same fervor as the first.

"SHE IS NOT MY FIRST pigeon."

"What's that mean?"

"Sponsors call the people they sponsor pigeons."

"You mean like Mark in a con."

"No dickhead, like a carrier pigeon. The only way to stay sober is to carry the message to other alcoholics."

"Sorry."

"For some alkies traumatic events like losing a sister. Someone who shares the same sponsor, dying in her arms could be traumatic enough to send her back to drink."

This woman was abrasive and tough, but her concern was clear.

Chapter 9

"**W**hat are you doing?" Eric had walked up behind Nya and startled her. She was looking for something in her purse.

"I am getting some money that I had with me.'

"Why?"

"Because you are going to send Brendan to the pizza place. I am starving to death and so are you. I heard your stomach growling all night." Nya had slept on the floor near Eric, afraid to be near any of the others and more afraid to let them know she was afraid.

She had noticed the way Calvin kept watching her. When she heard him speak, she knew the comment about fucking a nigger bitch has come from him.

Eric shielded his face in embarrassment. "Why Brendan?"

"Because Salvatore has the best pizza and by the time, he gets there it will be near noon. There is usually a bunch of kids his age picking up large pizza orders for the offices and the hospital."

"So, he will be invisible unlike if one of us was to walk in." Eric finished her thought.

"I also am going to take the bullet out of Jay. And I don't want him here for that."

Eric's face now had the stubble of days of growth and his eyes looked more tired than those he led. "We kidnapped you and threaten you and you are taking care of us. We have got to be the most pathetic bad guys in history."

Nurses do not remove bullets. It is a procedure done by doctors. Nya had lived in the swamp and knew about gunshots, snake bites, and delivering babies before she went to nursing school.

"Mushroom, onion, and cheese for me," Nya ordered handing some money to Eric.

Chapter 10

"Pay the man Wendell." Odela Dubois, Nya's mother requested as she stood in Wendell's doorway. She had been ubered from the airport after catching the first flight out after hearing her daughter had been kidnapped. Wendell had never met Odela Dubois so his mental image to a major hit when he saw the person now standing in his doorway. Odela was beautiful. She looked more like she should be Nya's sister than her mother. Both Nya and her mother had large-breasted curved bodies that could stop traffic. After Wendell paid the driver Odela hugged Wendell in such a way that it told him she was comforting him as much as he was comforting her on the missing of Nya. "My daughter sleeps in the same bed as you, correct.?" Wendell shook his head in confirmation, trying to suppress any feelings of guilt or embarrassment over their marital status or the lack thereof. "Lead me there."

Once in the bedroom, Odela began disrobing. "What are you doing."

"Oh, I am sorry I thought my daughter would have explained." She continued to remove her clothes.

"I am missing something." Wendell reached for her hand to stop her from removing her bra but missed stopping her and her bra hit the floor.

" I get readings on people and events. My clearest reading comes when I rest or sleep. I sleep in the nude."

"I understand then why don't we talk after you have rested." Wendell attempted to overt his eyes and her final garment flew away.

"Maybe we need to talk here and now." She sat on the bed and patted the bed for him to sit beside her. She picked up a pillow and covered herself. "Look, Wendell, I sleep in the nude and meditate in the nude, that is why I don't like hotels. I am getting older, and I don't always think about the sensitivities of the young such as yourself. I am pleased that a woman of my age can still give a young man such as yourself a woody. But this is not about sex. It is flattering. I did not mean to offend you, I just thought we both need to do all we can to get her back. It is your house, and you make the rules if you want me always dressed, I will comply. I am just scared for my baby." Odela seemed a little hurt that the shock of her openness stunned Wendell.

"NO, IT'S ME THAT NEEDS to apologize. I have got to have her back. We do whatever we can however we can. Rest now and we will talk later." Odela kissed him lightly on the forehead in a forgiving gesture then slid beath the covers.

"I was expecting a fat old woman in a turban," Wendell confessed as he left the room.

Chapter 11

"**S**tone bunch of screw-ups the lot of them. Got worse when that Eric fella got out of prison and got dumped here." Sheriff Grant explained.

After spending much of the morning reporting and reviewing what he had Lavon thought the best way to find Nya was to learn a little about Doris. Doris was from a trailer park somewhere near Logan Missouri, so he decided to drive there and check in with the local sheriff. "Crime in the area has gone down 90% since they left the area. You don't plan on sending them back anytime soon you." Sheriff Grant was an older man in a stained brown uniform. He looked like a prize fighter that may have spent too many years in the ring.

"I don't plan to send them back. Do you know where I could find Mrs. Fleischman? I don't know if there was an official notification on the death of her daughter?"

"She lives in that trailer park you passed through getting here but I am not sure which one. But if you go over to the coffee shop Loretta could tell you which trailer it is."

"Thank you, sheriff."

"ARE YOU THE GOOD COP or the bad cop?" Loretta was a perky blonde girl with a built-in smile and a button nose. She wore an impeccable uniform and had a bubbly personality.

"It's not like tv we are all a little of both."

"Well, you look like the good kind." She seated Lavon and brought him coffee and a roll.

"You see Reds Liquor store? Well, she drinks Canadian Ltd, and she loves those cookies with the white stuff in the middle." Loretta informed Lavon before giving him the trailer number.

"Remember that I served you coffee. One day I am going to be a big star in Hollywood."

"WELL THANK YOU, JESUS." The woman answering the door to the trailer welcomed Lavon. She stood in the light of the doorway wearing a sheer see-through slip. She had huge breasts the oversized nipples that impressed themselves on the material of her slip in such a way that they may have been making a permanent indentation. She was sun spotted and had red eyes from years of drinking and late nights. Her voice was graveled from years of smoking and her hair was a bundle of grey with some hint that it may have been red or orange at some point much earlier in her years.

"Are you Mona Fleischman?" Lavon asked just before being whisked into the trailer.

"All these years of being sent beat-up pot gut truckers. I mean it's all right if you are a trucker but some of these guys have a little trouble getting it up. I mean I can't raise the dead."

Lavon suppressed a chuckle and handed her the whiskey and the cookies.

"Let me get a couple of glasses."

"I won't be having any I got a long drive back."

Monna dropped ice into a rock glass and poured whiskey over it. She drank and the revitalization effect that came over her reminded Lavon of Roberta and her cigarettes.

"So, what is your pleasure? Strait, from the back in the back, or all the above."

Lavon showed her his badge.

"So, I've never been in Shepherds Pass."

"I am sorry to inform you that Dottie was killed yesterday." Monna finished the drink in the glass and Lavon poured her another. "Do you need more ice?" "Not unless you plan to build a fucking popsicle. I need more whisky."

After a silence followed by drinking followed by more silence and more drinking Mona asked. "Eric had something to do with this didn't he."

"That was one of the names the witness said she heard."

"The goddam Appleton Treasure."

"Can you explain?"

"The gang of them were just fuck up kids until Eric came along. He had just got out of prison with some cock and bull story about a treasure buried somewhere near here."

"Do you believe it's real?"

"I know it's real but what I don't know is if anyone will ever find it. But the group of them got mad to find that treasure."

"Buried treasure sounds like a myth."

"I overheard Eric one time say it was from a robbery years ago. Then it made sense some old person he knew in prison told him about the money being hidden but not were."

The drinking seemed to repair much of Mona's spirit.

"Tell me about Doris." Lavon requested.

"She was a good girl. But she was always too old for her year. She drank and turned a few tricks, but she worked taking care of old people through some agency, Bobcat staffing I think."

"What was she like as a little girl?"

Monna seemed glad about the question. "She was so great. She had one great friend Lamar Fulton."

"Was he one of the local boys?"

"No, he was a grown man. At first, I thought he might be a child molester but that wasn't it. He treated her like a daughter.

She never knew her father and somewhere he must have had a kid that wouldn't forgive him. So, they bonded. He was a magician who had fallen on hard times and began picking pockets to make ends meet. He had such a light touch he could put things into your pockets. He worked for the mob for a while setting up cops."

"Sounds like quite the role model."

"Look he loved her and taught her the trade. When I found out he was using her to rip off Johns, I stopped him from seeing her and shortly after he died of cancer. I don't think she ever forgave me for not letting her comfort her friend when he was dying."

This information gave Lavon an idea. He visited a little more until he was sure she would be alright.

"YOU'RE LATE." AN OLD man with a curved spin scowled at Lavon.

"Really."

"Yeah, truck loaders are already gone out. I can get you something sweeping the floor in a warehouse tonight if you just need the cash or if your parole officer is up your ass. No drinking, no screwing, and no stealing."

Lavon had walked into the Bobcat Staffing agency and found a short supply of people to send out on assignments. The room looked like a frontier classroom minus the little old schoolteacher. There were chalkboards covering the wall with doddles that meant something to someone.

"I'm a cop and I need your help."

"You aren't going to bust us."

"Gee, I hope not."

"Doris Dottie Fleischman went out on jobs for you. Look up the record of who her clients were."

"Look, cop what if she sues."

"Then she would have to do it from the great beyond."

"Oh. That kind of cop."

Chapter 12

"Sit up and let me change that bandage," Nya instructed Joey. "Yes ma'am," Joey said in a surly tone.

"Look, friend if every time I try to help you, you act like a smart ass you will only hurt yourself."

"Yeah, you're right. Sorry. Just still hurts a lot."

"I am going to give you some motion exercises to do, and I want you to do exactly what I tell you. Don't get macho on me and overdo or it will have the reverse effect that we are trying to get. Clear?"

"Your man must be a great guy to put up with such a spirited woman."

"I'm the lucky one."

Joey looked around to see if anyone could hear their conversation. "I need to tell you something."

Nya moved closer to Joey waiting to hear the worst.

"There was this thing we used to do with Doris. In the beginning, she was Scott's girl."

"What kind of thing?"

"We called it the game. We used to pass her around." Joey looked shocked that he had said it aloud.

"For sex?"

"Yeah, now I aint proud of what I did but I was just as much a part of it as anybody in the beginning."

"What changed?"

"She found AA or NA or the fucking PTA for all I know. All I know is that some such thing that made her have a change of mindset. That's why I am not sure why she ran off with the treasure." He paused. "I never touched her after she no longer wanted to play. But Calvin got off on her fighting and resisting. He like to choke her out until she passed out then he would bring her back around and start over."

"Joey. Why are you telling me this?"

"Because I see the way he is looking at you. I can't fight him off with a ripped shoulder and one arm."

"Joey, what do you suggest?"

"I see how much better Jay is doing. He's got color again and his breathing is much better. If he comes around and you get the chance, I think you should run for it."

"What?"

"I won't chase you and Eric is in your debt. So, you just must be sure Calvin or Brendan don't see you take off."

Nya looked at Joey for a moment and that was all it took for her to note his gratitude and sincerity.

"Brendan wants to someday be Calvin, so he is just as dangerous. I don't think I could stand to see them passing you back and forward."

"Won't Eric stop them?"

"Calvin has no allegiance to Eric other than the treasure."

"Again, with the treasure."

Joey reached into his pocket and pulled out a coin and handed it to Nya. It was a 1939 gold double eagle.

"Dottie dropped this when she was moving the treasure where we could not find it."

Nya's eyes were wide with amazement. "Oh, Shit."

"WE NEED TO TALK," NYA informed Eric. Nya had removed the bullet from his brother and Jay was resting. Nya was covered in sweat and blood, and she walked out to one of the loading doors for the abandoned truck terminal.

"Thank you. Whatever happens from here I know you did your best."

"We have another problem to fix."

"What's that?"

"Calvin."

"What about Calvin."

"I COULD NOT SLEEP LAST night because he was watching me. He watches me everywhere I go."

"Look."

"Look my ass, you said you were in prison you know his problem. He is some form of a sex addict. You also know the only way he is going to be able to rape me is to kill you and take over."

It was clear that Eric had already been thinking about Calvin's problem.

"What do you suggest?"

"Simple, we give him some money and let him get it off down in the hooker district."

Eric looked at her with surprise. "You think that will work?"

"Look Eric, you don't think you plan to set down roots in Shepherds Pass, it's a temporary solution, and if he keeps his mouth shut who would care? Look I have met a few of the girls from down there and I can recommend someone clean and that doesn't steal."

"Nya if I had met you before Doris, we would have that treasure and have been out of here by now."

Chapter 13

After Calvin had gone on his date Nya sat with Eric staring into the early evening. "When you were reading me what did you see?"

"What difference does it make you don't believe any of it."

"So, I still want to hear it."

"Okay but remember you asked. You are in love. You faked a breakup with the one you love for convenience."

"Go on."

"They are of the same gender as you." Nya stared at Eric wondering if she had crossed the line.

"When I was in the pen for the last time. There was this new guy. Someone beat him and raped him. He ended up in my cell. I cared for him, and we talked. Somewhere along the line, he had a sexual encounter. We both said it was just for then and that it did not change who we were and that when we got out life would go back as it had been."

"But something in the exchanges of love was more real than anything you have ever experienced before or after."

"Nya I am sharing a lot with you. If you pass the information along, I will have no choice but to kill you."

"Eric your health just like the health of Joey or Jay is important. I would not divulge anything we discussed. We made a deal."

"Whoever your man is he is the luckiest man on the planet." Eric assessed.

Eric walked away he did not bother to secure Nya. He knew she was bound by her words.

Chapter 14

"Are you two?" Agent Patterson began and before he confirmed that Lynn and Lavon were a couple Lynn answered.

"We are romantically involved. Let's avoid anything overly flattering or demeaning."

Lavon and Lynn had made reservations and were meeting Agent Patterson of the FBI and his wife Joan. Joan was Chinese American and surgeon at Shepherds Pass General. She had a sophisticated air about herself and an intelligent look about herself.

"Then aren't we the luckiest men on the planet with the most beautiful women." Patterson continued his compliment.

"Joan don't let these work horses fool you, I caught Lavon making plans to meet your husband here. The food is great, but I think the waitress are a little flirty for my taste."

Joan grabbed her husband's arm. "They had better back off this hunk is mine."

"What school did you go to.?" Lynn asked Joan.

"St. Louis University Medical School."

"I am going to speak at Washington University in a month or so. As a favor for Lavon's sister, she is organizing some sort of women in business discussions. I think it's in the same area."

"Well, if you need a tail gunner, I do lectures, and I would love to tag along."

"Sounds like winner."

Agent Patterson and Lavon sat staring at each other. "We came here to do a little business and these two are networking." Agent Patterson offered. The waitress came and brought the menus. "The Halibut and the Sea Bass are great." Lynn offered to Joan.
"It's a little high dollar."

"Well, it's on me and I have a bigger budget to work with than most at this table."

"I should be mad at you." Agent Patterson told Lavon.

"Why."

"First you give the country boy down home routine. I found out your father was the go-to ghost writer for retired cops and feds. Now he has a series of books of his own. Then I see you close 7 murders in the snap of your fingers."

"I got more than my finger snapped on that one."
"Why do FBI agents need a ghost writer?" Joan asked.
"Because after 30 years of writing only case reports everything you write reads like a Dragnet rerun." Agent Patterson remarked.
Everyone at the table laughed at the way the explanations were going.
"So, who is going to play me in the movie?"
Everyone stopped eating to stare at Agent Patterson.
"Babe don't hold out what movie?" Joan asked.
"Ask Lavon. He is writing the book." Patterson defended passing the folder had brought with him to Lavon.
"Speak country boy." Lynn commanded.

"Why don't we let Tim start off with the details." Lavon suggested.

"Aright back in the fifties four soldiers return home from Korean and decided to use their training to rob a bank. They screwed up and ended up with more money than they thought they would. There was an all-out blood bath. We believe that one of the bank robbers, Erwin Appleton, hid the money. Then went home and found his wife doing the horizontal boop with his next-door neighbor."

"Oh, my this does sound like and interesting tale." Lynn commented.

"Appleton kills the wife and the stud gets twenty years for the murder. Later he is connected to the robbery, before we can make a deal, he is in a prison incident and forgets how to tie his shoes."

Joan grabbed some the papers Lavon in looking at and starts to read. It was the medical side of the reports Agent Patterson had copied for the get together.

"Could he have been faking?" Lynn asked.

"No chance. I see the medical reports here he was lucky to be alive." Joan added.

"All the men are dead now. There have been agents all over the country trying to recreate their footsteps to find the loot but no luck. It has become known as the Appleton Treasure." Tim Patterson explained. "Later some warden realizes that Appleton should be up for parole. Appleton is using 20 times the average you would normally spend on medical care for an inmate. The warden notice that Appleton's parents died years ago and there is ample money to provide for his treatment privately. So, he pushes through the parole and puts him in the family estate with hot and cold running health care providers."

"How much we are talking, in regard to the treasure?" Joan asked.

"No one is quite sure." Lavon finally rejoined the conversation. "There was a bulk of gold double eagle coins and 1000.00 bill being taken out of circulation. So, we are talking about a half a billion dollars easy."

"And no one knows where it is" Tim stated.

"I wouldn't say no one knows." Lavon smiled.

"You are holding out on me again." Patterson proclaimed.

"I am looking for a missing person. Nya Dubois and I would sacrifice the money and let you collect it later if I can get her back safely.

"This is wrong on so many levels." Agent Patterson started. "You actually have the balls to blackmail the FBI in front of a Judge."

"Wait Tim I know Nya. It would break my heart if she was killed because we screwed up." Joan calmed her husband down.

"And please leave Lavon's ball out of the conversation. Their mine." Lynn commented and she and Joan laughed out loud.

"So, no book or movie?" Joan asked.

"No babe it looks like for now the FBI is on stand down until Lavon can get his friends girl back home."

"Then maybe we can decide who will play me." Joan interjected.

Chapter 16

"LOOK YOU GOT THE BLACK chick whether you two are screwing or not. Calvin gets to go out and get the hump of his lifetime and once again nobody think about me." Brendan as in full rant. "I get shot at. I go for pizza runs but when it comes to getting the real deal you want treat me like a little kid. Well fuck that."

"I was my fault." Nya confessed. " I thought that if I suggest that both of you go at the same time you might think it was a trap or a plan for me to escape. I was worried that you might overreact."

"Beside I made the final call and I stand by it. His needs outweighed yours." Eric proclaimed.

"I do know a girl, but she is rather young and hasn't been on the streets for long. I don't want anyone to hurt her." Nya began.

"Then she's the one. Please Eric. Look at the smile on Calvin's face. You can't deny me this."

"Her name is Sugar, and she hangs out near the Grand Hotel. Let me give you some money."

"HOW DID YOU PICK ME?" Sugar asked Brendan.

"A friend of yours, a Black girl a nurse."

Sugar lead Brendan into the dank poorly decorated motel room. She knew who had sent him and maybe it was a message. How could the girlfriend of the man she loved most in this world choose her to ask for help.

After having sex on the bed Sugar looked at Brendan noticing his eyes seemed to be memorizing her naked body. "I want you to do me a favor."

"The girl that recommended me lent me money. Give her back twenty. Can I trust you?"

"Sure. You know I always dreamed about being with a girl like you, Sugar."

"I have a fantasy too. Would you like to hear it."

"Yes, I would."

"Please don't make fun of me because it would hurt my feelings."

"Sure, what is your fantasy, Sugar."

"Well, I dropped out of high school, and I always wanted to be a cheerleader. And make it with a fine boy such as yourself right there in the bleachers."

"That sound like an interesting fantasy."

"Well, we change and go through life not knowing what is going to come up next but all we have are our memories. And that is the memory I would love to hold in my head forever."

Brendan began dressing.

"Could you be that boy?"

"What?"

"Tomorrow at midnight could you meet me at the high school field and rock my socks off. No charge but bring me a teddy bear. Doesn't have to be expensive just a keepsake."

"I could do that Sugar, but it has to be our secret."

"I bet tomorrow will be the best night of my life." Sugar squealed like an anxious teen.

Chapter 17

"Can I get you a cup of coffee?" Wendell offered Lavon. "No but if you still have some of the bottled water that would be great."

Wendell led Lavon into the kitchen. Before Lavon could turn around Odela charged Lavon and hugged him. She was completely naked shocking Lavon but causing Wendell to suppress a laugh.

"Jesus Christ lady."

"Lavon Tyler, may I introduce queen Odela Dubois, Nya's mother."

"Wow, now that beat the socks off any Mississippi greeting, I ever heard of."

"Sorry to shock you Lavon you now for two sexually active boys you seem quite regimented in your thinking." Odela stood close to Lavon with her hand on his chest.

"Would it be rude of me to ask why you are not wearing clothes ma'am?" Lavon asked.

"She gets her best insights without her clothes. "Wendell answered still suppressing a laugh.

"There I was naked sleeping in the bed the Wendell makes mad passional love to my daughter." Odela closed her eyes as if reliving the experience then made two fists and began thrusting her pelvis. Lavon and Wendell simultaneously began shaking their heads. "Then I saw her. Her mission is almost complete. She will be returning back to her bed of love."

"Mrs. Dubois." Wendell began.

"No, I think she has something." Lavon interjected trying to step back from the naked woman, but she would not remove her hand. "We got a dead body in one of the stolen cars and Abby shot a couple of others."

"So, you think she is there trying to save someone's life and won't leave until she knows if he is going to make it.' Wendell guessed.

"Her and her sisters are all very hardheaded. By the way Lavon, she is going to contact you. You must be receptive to the terms."

"Let's pretend I believe in this stuff. What terms?"

"I am but a humble messenger." Odela smiled and sashayed off.

"Buddy I would love to stick around her and help you with whatever this is that is going on around here, but I got damsels in distress to rescue."

"Chicken." Wendell muttered.

Chapter 18

"I have a message from the mayor." Sean Hardcastle had assembled the group in one of the conference rooms in the new police station. Lt Crawford sat silent waiting for the news Hardcastle was delivering to Lavon and the team of Lopez and Nash. "First the mayor said he loved your interview on the news. For the first time in recent history someone from this department came off as human and personally affected by a tragedy." Hardcastle noted adjusting in his chair. "Personally, I don't like anyone from this department saying anything other than no comment on the news unless cleared by my office. I want to know tomorrow's news today." Hardcastle was public relations manager for the mayor's office. "But you made the little chick look stupid having no way to slam you without looking heartless herself. So, no victim no crime as they say." Hardcastle shuffled some papers. "I have seen the dailies on both recent major crimes, the shoot out and the abduction and you think they are connected. So, what's the goal?" Hardcastle stared directly at Lavon.

"It's a bloody treasure hunt."

"What, that's stupid."

"With all due respect sir. I had dinner with an FBI agent that says they have been looking for the missing money from a heist that took place around fifty years ago."

"No chance for your daily yet, son." Lt Crawford cleared her throat as if referring to Lavon as son might taint the meeting. "How much are they guessing?"

"Over a half billion dollars in adjusted us dollars. Some in gold double eagles."

"Ouch." Nash screamed.

"And we got the jump on the FBI?" Lopez beamed.

"The recovery of the missing girl is my primary concern. Finding the money is the easy part." Lavon confessed.

"For the love of God, Son as your Lieutenant refers to you, please focus." Hardcastle admonished.

"Sir the Lt and my father are old friends, and she sometimes refers to me that way to keep me in line. Since my own partner refers to me as hillbilly, I find Son goes down a lot smoother." Lavon smiled at the Lieutenant. "But the truth is if those guys find the money, they may kill any loose ends." Lavon explained.

"Sir you also need to understand that if this information leaves the room at an inopportune time people could be out digging up all of Shepherds Pass. Gold Fever is real. People will kill each other for a shot at a half billion." Nash added to Lavon's thought. "We could have neighbors shooting each other for digging up the other guy's lawn."

"Sir we need to keep this under control a little longer and since both investigations have intersected, we need to be working with Lavon and Abby." Lopez added noticing the surprise that came over Lavon's face as she included Abby as an active participant of the investigation.

AS LAVON RETURNED TO his desk, he noticed a young girl sitting in the guest chair waiting for him. When he walked closer, he recognized her as it was Sugar. "I got a message for you."

"From Nya?"

"Look at my arm I'm breaking out in a rash. Police stations no matter how nice do that to me. Can we go somewhere else and talk?" Sugar should Lavon red blotches that were appearing. Shepherds Pass Police had recently moved into a newly build building.

"I would like a walk by the lake. We can feed the ducks."

"You're still as nice as I first thought. Let's go." Sugar bounced out of the chair as if a great adventure has been laid at her feet.

"I GOT TO TELL YOU FIRST."

"You have terms?" Lavon guessed as they walked along the manmade lake feeding the ducks.

"I was going to say conditions, but terms do sound nicer."

"How did Nya contact you?"

"She sent me a message sort of. She sent me a guy to have sex with. I guess he is one of the ones that is holding her."

"Any Idea as to her condition?"

"No but he doesn't seem like the kind that would hurt her, but I don't know about his friends."

"Where is she?"

"So here is where we talk terms. First, I am going to meet with the guy that I had sex with, but you won't arrest him."

"You don't want him to know you set him up?"

"No, he is a kid. When we had sex, he had love in his eyes. I aint going to shatter that. Besides maybe I might want to meet him somewhere in the future and start a friendship."

"Okay, good enough we follow or track him."

"You are good at making deals. Next when I meet up with him, we are going to have sex and you cannot interrupt."

"Sugar please."

"Sorry all terms on nonnegotiable. He might go away for twenty years, and he need to remember the last piece of ass he had for a long time."

Lavon put his arm around Sugars shoulder knowing she was leaving the hardest term of all for last.

"You can't take Wendell."

"Why because you love Wendell."

Sugar held her face down to stop Lavon from looking directly at her. "What did I forget to wash it off my face this morning."

"Sugar, no one is making fun of you. I knew when we first met that he was special to you. And I know you are special to him; your lives just don't match. But that doesn't mean you can't care about each other."

Sugar hugged Lavon.

"Thank you for not making my feeling seem like a dirty joke. Don't let him be there. He will kill someone. It's bad enough that I am risking myself to return another woman to his bed. And the saddest thing is she must know how I feel about him, and she still sent a message to me."

Lavon and Sugar walked the lake until she felt better, then they had lunch. She explained how she would be meeting Brendan.

Chapter 19

"Cletus, your father is home." Abby called to let Lavon into her small apartment. The apartment was in a mess. It was evident that the puppy had been pulling things out and Abby saw no need to clean up behind him. Cletus peaked his head out of the bedroom, he had a lace bra in his mouth dragging it. "Kid likes to play hid in seek in my underwear drawer."

"He is making a mess."

"Well pulling stuff out seems to relax him. He has had a traumatic experience. Maybe some time I will teach him to clean. But I think he is too young to run the vacuum cleaner and his legs are too short to reach the sink to wash the dishes." She picked him up and put him on the table. "I took him to the vet for shots and they want to cut his dick off."

"It's called neutering."

"Have you ever had a dog."

"Yes, my brothers and I raised hounds for a while for tracking."

"So was your dog neutered."

"No, he was used for breeding purposes."

Abby covered Cletus ears. "Don't let our son here you were a doggie pimp."

"Abby I am here to let you know you are reinstated. The Lieutenant says if you need a few days take it."

"So let me ask. Did you have a pink Lincoln and wear a big fuzzy hat? And Did you wear a cape with platform shoes." Abby laughed and Cletus licked her face.

"I need to ask you some questions about AA."

"Sure, the second A stands for anonymous."

"Not necessarily about a person but how the members view the program."

"Sure." Abby looked more like she was willing to help.

"If someone in AA came up with a large amount of money that was stolen why wouldn't run off with it?"

"Rigorous honesty. The backbone of the program."

"I don't understand."

"We must be honest to stay sober. The person might feel to compromise would jeopardize their sobriety."

"But they could work for a staffing agency the cheated or evaded taxes."

"Oh, now I see where you are confused. The saying on the chips we collect says to thy own self be true. So, we are honest but not on a crusade to force others to accept our view of honesty."

"Something else just occurred to me. I have been walking around and most of the time I collect the small pieces until I make up the big picture. This time I keep seeing the big picture and missing the small stuff."

"I don't get it."

"I miss having my partner to discuss thing with even if she is a pain in the ass. Abby, I need you to pull it together. We got a shot at bringing that girl home and I need you."

Abby sat there holding Cletus for a moment then look up with tears in her eyes.

"I keep washing my hair. But I can't get the smell out. The smell of brain matter. She was enough like me to be my sister and all I got left if the smell of her in my hair."

"Abby I am so sorry we all have been treating you like a cop and forgetting you are a victim as well." Lavon hugged Abby.

"I told the vet that I would rather he cut your dick off."

Lavon chucked.

"Don't laugh your appointment is next Wednesday."

Chapter 20

Lavon and Abby were hidden in dugout area where they could view the bleachers. Nash and Lopez were hidden behind the groundkeeper's shed. Both groups were connected by two-way radio and watched through binoculars. Lavon wanted Sugar and Brendan to feel that they were alone. Right on time Brendan walked up to the bleacher carrying a small teddy bear. Brendan looks small and lost. he looked around be sure no one was watching.

"I recognize that one." Abby confirmed.

"Alright team two we have a positive ID on the suspect on the field." Lavon whispered into the radio.

"Copy that." Nash acknowledged.

"This is so wrong." Lopez whispered to Nash.

In second Sugar can walking across the football field. She was wearing a cheerleader skirt. Walked up to Brendan and did a cheer kicking her legs up high and revealing she wore no panties.

"IS LAVON REALLY GOING to make us watch this?" Lopez stated.

"Is it me or is it hot out here?" Nash responded.

SUGAR RAN TO BRENDAN and jumped wrapping her legs around his waist then pushing him back onto one on the benches in the bleachers. In an instant she was riding him.

LAVON NOTICED ABBY slid her hands down the front of her pants. "Abby, you can't do that." He whispered.

"This whole porno rodeo is your idea so help or turn your head it's up to you."

LOPEZ TOOK HER GAZE off the young couple having sex in the bleachers for a moment and looked over at Lavon and Abby's position. "OH my god is she really doing that?"

"Wow." Nash comment as he made out Abby pleasuring herself. "Lavon that poor bastard."

"Poor me. You're married or I be touching you in a big way." Lopez remarked.

"HOW LONG CAN THEY KEEP this up?" Lavon remarked as Brendan and Sugar changed positions for the fourth time in forty-five minutes.

FINALLY, SUGAR DID a half walk half skip back down the football field as Brendan stood there watching her blend into the night. Making no attempt to stop the magic of the spinning in his head to slow down.

"Are you finished." Lavon asked Abby after it was clear she had peaked. She whipped her hands on his jacket and spoke.

"Now I am."

"Great now I have to burn this sports jacket before I can go home."

"Hey, Lavon you sure know how to throw a steak out." Lopez called into the radio.

The two teams had no problem following Brendan back to the trucking terminal. Lavon spotted Nya walking about the terminal checking the injured men.

Chapter 21

"Are you Erics girl?" A scratchy whispered voice called out to Nya. Nya was so happy to hear Jays voice.

"You gave your brother quite a scare." She began dabbing his face with a wet towel.

"Did Dottie tell you where she hid the treasure?" Nya tried not to meet his gaze. "Why don't I let your brother bring you up to date." Nya hoped she had not caused alarm by not answering his questions.

"How soon before he can be moved?" Eric asked.

"I don't recommend moving him anytime soon, he needs to be in a hospital. I have monitored his temp and blood pressure and he may not be showing signs of infection or sepsis but without whole blood to work with he will be week for a while."

"Are the two of you in love?" Jay whispered.

"She's your nurse not my girl." Eric answered looking more at Nya than his brother.

"Shame. She has a lot of concern in her voice."

"WE NEED TO TALK ABOUT how we get you back where you belong." Eric stated.

"Go and leave him with me. I will take care of him." Nya suggested.

"That sounds good, but I am going for the gold. I got to find the lady cop that shot us to shit and even things out."

"Eric please don't."

"Look cancel that witch shit. You can't look through me."

"Eric I am going to tell you something and you had better listen to me. My fiancée is a Cop and by the description of the woman you guys had a run in with you will lose big time. She is a drunken physio and damn good at killing."

"Nya you can't save me."

"Think about your lover he will be crushed, and you will never get the chance to explain how all the stuff you said before you left him meant nothing."

"The drunken cop can only do me a favor. I been in prison most of my life and I aint going back. Its beaches and white sand or a whole in the ground all the same to me."

"Then fuck you, Eric."

"Watch your mouth."

"Fuck you for being my friend and protecting me." As Nya turned her back and walked away, she did not care if she had pushed Eric too far.

IN AN ACTIVE SHOOTER or hostage rescues the first team in is not the rescue team but the kill team. The kill team has the job of eliminating the threat. Usually these are specialized police that are ready to do whatever is necessary to eliminate the any person or persons they think may cause a hazard to the success of the operation.

The entry team leader looked at Lavon. " One last time to back out. My boys are tough. Our moto is we kill shit."

"No, she's my responsibility I go with the entry team."

Abby looked at Lavon as if there was something she wanted to say but just stared at Lavon.

There were three separate explosions that came so close together that they sounded like one. Glass shattered and flew as a group of police in tactical gear burst into the room carrying automatic weapons. Calvin and Brendan ran for an exit but were tackled and brought to the ground and handcuffed by officers. Joey stood and tried to run off, but he was quickly collected.

"Careful with his arm that is some of my best work." Nya called out.

Eric stepped from behind corner holding a .357 pointing it at Lavon. Lavon could see a sharpshooter pointing a rife at Eric.

"Don't shoot." Nya called out and walked in front of Eric.

"Nya step out of the way." Lavon instructed.

"No, Lavon his gun is empty he is trying to commit suicide with your help." Nya took her hand out of her pocket and dropped six bullets on the floor.

"The witch says you don't die today." She placed her right hand in the center of his chest and took his gun from his hand and handed it to Lavon. Two officers rushed over to handcuff Eric.

"I don't get it how did you unload my gun." Eric stared at Nya as if he had witnessed magic.

"I didn't, the bullets came from your brother's gun, yours is still loaded. Sometimes a little believing is all I need." Nya smiled and walked away.

Outside Abby walked up to Lavon when she was sure no one could hear then. "Look meathead in the future no more of that cowboy crap. Leave the kill team burst through the door shit to the guys that do this on a regular basis."

"Nice to have you back Abby." Lavon smiled and walked away to prepare for the next phase of his plan.

Chapter 22

Lavon and Abby walked into the Dodd storage with Nash and Lopez and accompanied by Lynn and FBI agent Patterson. The thin man with middle eastern feature stood behind the counter.

"Always on my night to work." The man said.

"What does that mean?" Lavon asked.

"It means that anything crazy always happen on my night to work never on my brothers. I am Ahmed how can I help you,"

"Show us where Dottie Fleishman's storage locker is." Abby asked.

"Why you are not her."

Abby handed Ahmed; Dottie's will signed in the hospital. "I don't know if this is legal." Ahmed stated.

"It is." Lynn offered.

"Are you a lawyer, lady?"

"Well yes and a Judge."

"Always on my night. And who is this?" He asked Agent Patterson.

"Agent Patterson FBI."

"Always on my night, follow me." He led them to the locker.

"Do we need a crowbar?" Patterson asked.

"No. I have the key." Lavon reached into his pocket and took out the key that had fallen out of Abby's purse.

"Lynn, this man of your is always holding out on me. He had the loot for days but would not budge." Patterson offered causing Lynn to smile.

"My case was Nya. She is back and we are assisting on Lopez and Nash's case." Lavon opened the heavy storage locker door and filled up to the ceiling was all forms of riches. There were boxes of thousand-dollar bills and gold coins everywhere. The was a tablet and paper where Doris had been trying to count the amount.

"That jerk. She didn't want to steal the money from the crew, she wanted to turn it in and split the finder's fee. That still would have made them rich. The clown was too honest to tap into the money to pay her rent, so she died owning me." Abby said more to the room than any one person. Two police cruisers showed up to cart the money off, but more were called in to help.

"We want our money back, Lavon." Patterson stated, this made the crowed laugh. "So how did you know where it was?"

" Dottie's mother gave me the clue. She said that Dottie was a pick pocket and sleight of hand specialist. She could plant things on people with the best of them."

"That creep she put the key in my purse when she was putting the dog in the car." Abby realized.

"How did you know which storage company?" Patterson asked

"There are only three in driving distance. One used electric key paid, one swipes and this one uses a key. I checked them all out when I first moved here."

" Needed extra space for your extra banjos and your butter churn no doubt." Abby joked.

"So why didn't she take off?" Patterson asked.

"Rigorous honest. It would have been stealing and she only wanted to die sober. She was storing it here until she could work out a finder's fee. Probably had trouble counting up a current value." Abby stated.

"Now I am lost how did see get it in the first place?" Lynn asked.

"Eric was in prison with Appleton and probably researched his story and found out about the money. But Appleton was too far gone to know where he put it." Lavon offered.

"I still don't get it." Lynn stated.

"Well Eric had Doris Dottie go to work for Appleton changing his adult diaper and scrubbing behind his balls." Nash started.

"Somewhere during all that ball washing Appleton thinks back to a wife or girlfriend who did the same for him in his younger days. Presto out comes where he hid the loot. She probably had more trouble moving it than finding it." Lopez speculated.

"So how do I get the money back where it belongs, with the Fed?" Patterson asked.

"Finder's fee." Lavon remarked.

"You are cops you can't claim a finder's fee."

"No but the equivalent can be donated to Shepherds Police. We need new cars." Lavon stated.

Vinita Gonzalez ran up almost tripping on her stilettos with a cameraman in tow.

"Wow this is going to make great news." She eyed the Treasure. "I just left the hospital interviewing Nya." She ran over and put her arm round Lavon's waist. Lynn grabbed Vinita's arm and removed it "No touching."

Chapter 23

"Nya accepted Wendell proposal finally so be ready for a wedding." Lavon and Lynn lye rested in bed. "Her mother walks around the house in the nude."

"During the visit?"

"Yeah. I guess it's going to be a real tough place for Wendell when her sisters and her mother are all prancing through the house bare ass naked. Visiting when it's time for the wedding is going to be quite a spectacle." Lavon remarked. "I guess being his friend if he needs some help, I will have to...."

"You will just stay your ass right here in this bed mister. And what was all the gratitude from the news lady?"

"The fire department guy told me that there is war between the cops and the news people. After a talk with the mayor's public relations guy, I know why."

"So, you are trying to build some friendship capital for future use?"

" If we don't, they are destined to make us look like jack asses."

"Are you still moving out?"

"Noreen says I was not being quite fair not making the decision with you."

"Score one for the Tyler women."

"I realized how much I enjoy waking up next you when Nya was missing."

"Please stay. You help me heal too."

Chapter 24

N ya sat down in a small chair with a phone. There was a bullet proof glass between her and the person she had come to see. "Do I know you." he grunted.

"Eric sent me."
"Why?"

"He wanted to apologize for causing a false argument. He was afraid you could move on, and he could not."

The inmate said nothing.

"What now."

"He says meet him at the ranch in time." I don't know what that means but he says you will.

"Did he ever find the treasure?"

"He came close, but someone stood in his way and the cop got the treasure."

"So, it was real."

"Watch the news. It was real. I left a gift on your account."

"Why?"

"Because Eric protected me when I needed it most and that is something I think he got from loving you."

Nya stood and walked away.

Just as it has been the duty of lighthouses for hundreds of years to guide ships safely into harbors. Thank you for allowing us at the Looking Glass Lighthouse to steer your thoughts dreams and imagination safely to a port of enjoyment.

We are pleased that you have chosen to join us on this journey.

Please feel free to send feedback, questions, and comments to Lookingglasslighthouse@gmail.com and be sure to make your preferred literature vendor aware of your experience.

AS A SPECIAL THANK you for allowing us to entertain you we would like to give you a special sneak peek into the next episode of Shepherds Pass- Robinhood in Shepherds Pass

Chapter 1

There are as many variations of the tale of Robin Hood as there have been actors who have played the role on stage and in cinema. The central premise, however, remains the same. Robin Hood was a criminal or highwayman who stole from the rich to give to the poor. A deadly game of Robin Hood would unfold in Shepherds Pass's early fall. This game would alter, test, or end the lives of those involved.

Mr. John Ashworth Sr. helped his wife empty the car of groceries. As they entered their small, modest home, Mrs. Ashworth went to close the door behind herself, and something blocked it. More accurately, someone. A man in a dark suit pushed the door open so hard that Mrs. Ashworth hit the floor. Mr. Ashworth dropped the groceries he had been carrying. A broad woman with an evil stare stood behind the man eyeing the fallen Mrs. Ashworth.

"You must be John Ashworth." The large man confirmed.

"Who are you?" Trembling, Mr. Ashworth asked.

"Well, in this case, you could say I am the Sherriff of Nottingham, and I am here to see Little John.

Another man walked in from the back room. He had broken into the rear of the house. "Kids not here."

"Well, we still have work to do." The Sheriff of Nottingham announced. "You, sir, are what's wrong with this country. You raise your children not only to show you no respect but to disrespect others and their rights and property."

Mr. Ashworth looked confused. The Sheriff of Nottingham punched him in the gut so hard Ashworth lost all his wind. He doubled over in pain. Ms. Ashworth reached out to plea with the man beating her husband, for she knew the beating had just begun. But the stocky woman slapped Mrs. Ashworth so hard she flew over a coffee table.

"These kids hack and steal everything that isn't nailed down. The government doesn't stop them. The few they catch get slaps on the wrist. Well, I came here to slap your wrist a little." The men took turns beating Mr. Ashworth as the woman beat and kicked his wife.

"Now, let's go find little John. I hope the PI is worth the money." The man representing himself as the Sheriff of Nottingham said, straightening out his tie in a broken, bloody mirror in the now ransacked home of the Ashworth's before leaving.

Chapter 2

"Code Blue. Second shift surgical team to emergency room stat. Code Blue. Surgical scrub team to emergency room stat." The automated disembodies voice called out. Then repeated it several times.

"Shit. I thought I would make it to the end of the shift without trouble." Joan Patterson, a surgeon at Shepherds Pass General Hospital, murmured more to herself than anyone in the cafeteria. She threw the half Danish she had been gnawing on in the trash and dumped her coffee and fast walked toward the emergency room. On her way, she saw Flash. Flash was the nickname for the anesthetic that was on duty. Flash was known for his 100-yard dash speed. He shot past Joan leaving a vibration in his wake. Good, she thought. I love the enthusiasm of that guy. Flash was a thin black man of medium complexion with thin-rimmed glasses who looked like he should be posing for a runner's magazine even when standing still. Joan knew she was irritable due to missing her husband. Tim Patterson is an FBI agent assigned to Shepherds Pass, and lately, they had been working shifts that had caused them to end out sleeping during different hours, if not missing each other entirely.

When Joan reached the reception desk, the first thing she noticed was that Flash was highly agitated. The reception desk was manned by Theresa, a temporary worker that had been brought in to cover regular personal, exercising earned leave.

"What's the problem, Flash? Where's our patient?" Joan asked over the repeated code blue call.

"This idiot says there is none," Flash answered.

"Watch who you call an idiot, you skinny little fool. I can bounce you off the walls." Wanda was a black woman of a much darker complexion than Flash. She wore long fake nails in an outlandish glowing shade. Wanda had false eyelashes that appeared four inches long and curled with clumps of whatever glue was used to bind them to her natural eyelashes. She was huge in a loose fat way and wore long hair extensions that did not in the slightest resemble human hair.

"What?" Joan struggled to wrap her mind around what was going on. She knew Flash to be quiet and reserved. Now here he was in full strike mode.

"Lady, shut that God Damn automated thing off." Joan finally yelled.

"Look, you doctors can't talk to people any way you want. I am a person too." Wanda defended.

"Look, lady, it's your communication system that is calling out the troops. Shut it down." Flash now seemed upset with himself for losing his cool.

Wanda reached over and turned off the switch on the panel that controlled the automated help beacon. "I never touched it. It went off by itself."

"Since you did not have an emergency, didn't it occur to you to turn it off?" Flash asked, trying to regain his composure, but Wanda's disregard was apparent, and Joan felt bad for Flash for having to acquiesce.

"Code Blue all available surgical and scrub teams to intensive care stat." The automated beacon screamed and repeated it. Flash and Joan turned and walked fast toward intensive care without a word. Before reaching the room, Flash spoke. "I am sorry, Doctor Patterson. I didn't mean to lose my cool back there. I know if a team member is seen as out of control, it reflects badly on you."

"No apology necessary, Flash. I wanted to slap the fat ass bitch myself." Joan smiled, and her candor relieved Flash. When Flash and Joan reached intensive care, it was like a staff meeting. The room was full of people wondering why they had been called there. Joan looked down at the watch and remembered it was Thursday. She had jeopardized time with her husband for whatever this malarkey was. She reached over a grabbed an aluminum bedpan. She angrily walked from the room with all eyes watching her.

"Doctor Patterson. Please don't do something stupid. I know it's not my place, but please just stop for a minute and think." Flash followed behind Joan, trying to calm her down. Joan saw a gurney with a body completely covered being wheeled from one of the rooms in her route. Joan stopped and pulled back the sheet covering the man's face. "What happened?" Joan asked the nurse wheeling the man.

"Not sure. The emergency buzzer should have gone off. He was on a drip to keep him stable. The drip stopped, but the alarm never went off. We went for a check, and he was stone-cold dead. I hate whatever is happening to the alarms around here. People are dying, and no one even wants to talk about it." The event clearly moved the nurse. Joan turned and walked even more angrily than before. She reached the IT department. "Who is in charge here?" Joan asked, and a lanky man in a bow tie raised his hand. Joan jumped on his desk and began hitting him with the bedpan. Joan is a small woman of Asian descent, and Flash knew it was his job to restrain her, but he felt uncomfortable even touching a married woman due to his strict upbringing. Flashes timidity caused the bedpan beating to persist longer than it should have. Finally, the security team was able to handcuff Joan and call the Shepherds Pass police.

AND JUST IN CASE YOU have not yet had a seek peek into Noreen Tyler A Tyler Girl Adventure

Chapter one

Bailey slowing walked across the pool area. It was early fall in St. Louis and the weather was mild. Bailey wore only a towel that she had wrapped around herself. She a carried an open bottle of wine in one hand and a glass in the other. The neighborhood was one of St. Louis's gated places with a private street. It was night and she felt sad. Bailey had just finished making love but it in no way sufficed to cure the aching she felt. She had run the risk of hurting Simon. Bailey looked toward the main house resisting the urge to burst open the back doors that were never locked and throw herself on Simon's mercy. The fight had been her fault she knew it. How could she dare to challenge his love for her. He had filled so many voids that she never thought could never be filled. Even her parents had no comprehension of what Simon meant to her. "Oh, my poor Simon." She thought. "Probably in one of those creative trances. I'll beg your forgiveness in the morning." Bailey walked to the hot tub and dropped her towel. She looked down for a moment admiring her body. She was nineteen and had greater than perfect body. Even women who modeled had the tendency to be mushy in areas. Sports made her firm and strong. She lye back in the hot tub and enjoyed her wine. There was a sound of music coming from the guest house and music started to play louder as the guest house door open.

"Oh, look we don't want to talk about it anymore. It was great but all good things come to an end." Bailey uttered just before being shot three times in the chest. Her eyes opened wide in astonishment. Was she shocked to be leaving life or shocked to be entering into whatever comes next. There was no asking her now.

Chapter 2

"**W**ill you please cover her up, I beg of you for the umpteenth time." Simon Garrett had found the body. He had contacted the police and now a detective Earnest Shockley stood before him. Shockley was a solid looking man in his mid-fifties wearing a suite that look long past its expiration date. He had a military hair cut that showed a fair amount of grey. Shockley, scribbled on a note pad and looked around as if anyone asking him a question should know not to expect an answer.

"Just a few questions, Professor."

"Don't call me Professor. I am a writer I don't teach anymore." Simon corrected.

"Mr. Garrett how is it you found the body in the morning. Didn't you miss her not coming back to bed?"

"That's a stupid question filled with inferences. I choose not to answer." Simon was agitated to the point of being ill.

"Look Professor she is young enough to be your kid. Hell, she is young enough to be your grandkid the way things go these days. You must see my position there has got to be some hard questions asked and it's my job to be the one asking those questions."

"I don't understand."

"Was she cheating on you for a younger guy is that why you shot her?"

"Leave and that the cheap suite with you. You will be speaking to my lawyer." Simon wandered back into the house and collapsed on the sofa.

Don't miss out!

Visit the website below and you can sign up to receive emails whenever Alex Mitchell publishes a new book. There's no charge and no obligation.

https://books2read.com/r/B-A-UGUAB-MEXOC

BOOKS 2 READ

Connecting independent readers to independent writers.

Also by Alex Mitchell